Fragments of Justice

Lieutenant Dundy

Published by Lieutenant Dundy, 2023.

FRAGMENTS OF JUSTICE

First edition. May 10, 2023.

Copyright © 2023 Lieutenant Dundy.

ISBN: 979-8223488453

Written by Lieutenant Dundy.

Table of Contents

Chapter 1: The Desperate Call

The rain-soaked city streets glistened under the flickering neon lights, casting an eerie glow on the faces of desperate souls. In the heart of this labyrinthine metropolis, where shadows whispered secrets and sins were bartered like currency, Sam Spade, a hardened private investigator, prowled the dark alleys in search of truth.

His office, a dimly lit room that reeked of stale cigarette smoke and regret, was a sanctuary for those who dared to cross the thin line between right and wrong. Sam's name had become synonymous with justice in a city where justice had a price tag, and everyone had something to hide.

With a fedora pulled low over his piercing eyes and a trench coat billowing behind him, Sam walked the treacherous tightrope between law and chaos, drawn to the underbelly of society like a moth to the flame. He was no stranger to the twisted minds that lurked in the shadows, for he had his own demons to battle.

The phone rang, its shrill cry cutting through the heavy silence of the office. Sam's hand moved instinctively, grabbing the receiver as if it held the key to salvation. On the other end, a desperate voice whispered of betrayal, danger, and a web of deceit that threatened to unravel lives.

As Sam listened to the desperate voice on the other end of the line, a shiver ran down his spine. The words painted a picture of treachery and danger, weaving a web of deceit that threatened to entangle innocent lives. He knew he couldn't turn away from this call for help, not when lives hung in the balance.

"Who is this?" Sam's voice was a low growl, laced with a mixture of determination and caution.

"Sam, it's Elena," the voice replied, filled with fear and urgency. "I need your help. They're coming for me. I've stumbled upon something big, something that could expose the entire underworld. But they'll do anything to silence me."

Sam's mind raced. Elena was a journalist known for her fearless pursuit of the truth. She had a knack for digging up dark secrets and exposing corruption. If she was involved, then whatever she had uncovered must have been significant.

"Where are you, Elena?" Sam asked, his voice steady.

"There's a safe house on 7th Street, apartment 303," Elena whispered, her voice trembling. "Please, Sam, you're my only hope. They'll kill me if they find me."

"I'll be there," Sam assured her, his jaw set. "Stay hidden, Elena. Trust no one."

As Sam hung up the phone, he knew that this case would be unlike any other he had encountered. The stakes were higher, the shadows deeper. He reached for his hat, pulling it lower over his eyes, and buttoned up his coat. The rain tapped against the windowpane, matching the urgency pounding in his chest.

The hunt had begun, and Sam Spade was determined to follow the trail of breadcrumbs through the maze of gritty urban landscapes, exposing the darkness that festered beneath the surface. In the realm of crime noir, where shadows held secrets and trust was a luxury, Sam Spade was a sentinel of truth, ready to face the demons that others dared not confront.

Little did he know that this twisted tale would push him to his limits, challenging his beliefs and unveiling a truth more sinister than he could have ever imagined.

Chapter 2: The Thin Line

The rain continued to pour relentlessly as Sam made his way through the dimly lit streets towards the safe house on 7th Street. Every step brought him closer to the heart of the mystery that had ensnared Elena and threatened to unravel the delicate balance between order and chaos.

The city at night had a different energy, an undercurrent of danger that pulsed through its veins. Sam's footsteps echoed against the wet pavement, the sound a reminder of the path he had chosen. He couldn't help but ponder the thin line he walked between being a guardian of justice and succumbing to the darkness he sought to eradicate.

As he approached the rundown apartment building, Sam noticed a flickering neon sign nearby, casting an eerie glow on the rain-soaked pavement. It read "Lucky's Bar," a notorious watering hole known for attracting the city's underworld. The bar had its own secrets, and Sam couldn't ignore the possibility that it held a connection to Elena's predicament.

Taking a detour, Sam pushed open the creaking door of Lucky's Bar and stepped into the smoky haze that engulfed the room. The air was heavy with the scent of alcohol and desperation, as weary souls sought refuge in liquid courage. Sam scanned the dimly lit room, his eyes sharp, searching for any familiar faces or clues that could lead him closer to the truth.

At the far end of the bar, a figure slouched on a stool, nursing a drink. The man's disheveled appearance and the haunted look in his eyes hinted at a troubled past. Intrigued, Sam approached, taking the seat next to him.

"Mind if I join you?" Sam asked, his voice neutral.

The man glanced at Sam, a mix of suspicion and resignation etched on his face. "Suit yourself," he muttered, his voice tinged with weariness.

Sam ordered a drink, and as he took a sip, he studied the man beside him. There was a familiarity in the way he carried himself, a haunted air that echoed Sam's own demons. Sensing a potential connection, Sam decided to test the waters.

"You look like a man who's seen his fair share of trouble," Sam remarked, his voice low.

The man's eyes met Sam's, guarded yet curious. "You have no idea," he replied cryptically.

"Names Sam," Sam introduced himself, extending a hand.

The man hesitated for a moment before shaking Sam's hand. "Call me Jack," he said, his grip firm.

As the two men exchanged cautious glances, a silent understanding passed between them. They were both seekers of truth, wandering souls in a city that thrived on secrets. Jack's troubled past held clues that could shed light on Elena's predicament, and Sam knew that uncovering the truth required alliances in unexpected places.

Sam leaned in closer, his voice barely above a whisper. "I'm searching for a woman named Elena. She's in danger, and I believe her life is connected to something big, something that threatens to expose the underbelly of this city."

Jack's eyes widened, a flicker of recognition passing through them. "Elena... I've heard the name. She was sniffing around, digging up things she shouldn't have. Word on the street is that she got too close to something dangerous."

Sam's heart quickened. "Do you know anything more? Anything that could help me find her?"

Jack hesitated, his gaze shifting as if weighing the consequences of revealing too much. Finally, he spoke, his voice filled with caution. "There's a man... a powerful figure in the criminal underworld. They call him 'The Baron.' If Elena stumbled upon something big, it's likely that she crossed paths with him. The Baron operates from the shadows, manipulating the strings that control the city's underworld."

Sam's eyes narrowed, his mind racing with the newfound information. The Baron was a name that sent chills down the spines of even the most hardened criminals. He was known for his ruthlessness and his ability to remain untouchable, always staying one step ahead of the law.

"Do you have any idea where I can find this Baron?" Sam pressed, his voice filled with determination.

Jack leaned in closer, his voice barely audible over the raucous noise of the bar. "There's a warehouse on the outskirts of town, an old industrial district. Rumor has it that it serves as The Baron's headquarters. But be careful, Sam. The Baron doesn't take kindly to those who meddle in his affairs."

Sam nodded, gratitude mingled with caution in his expression. He knew that stepping into The Baron's territory would be like diving into a den of vipers, but he had a debt to repay and a woman to save. He couldn't afford to back down now.

As Sam rose from his seat, preparing to leave Lucky's Bar, he extended a hand towards Jack. "Thank you for your help. If there's anything else you remember or if you hear anything about Elena, don't hesitate to reach out."

Jack nodded, a flicker of something akin to hope crossing his weary face. "I'll keep my ears open, Sam. Just be careful out there. The Baron is not someone to be taken lightly."

With those words of caution lingering in the air, Sam made his way back into the rain-soaked night. The warehouse on the outskirts of town beckoned him like a dark specter, its secrets waiting to be unraveled. The path ahead was treacherous, fraught with danger, but Sam knew that he had no choice but to confront The Baron and unearth the truth that lay buried beneath layers of deceit.

Chapter 3: Shadows of Betrayal

The rain poured relentlessly as Sam approached the outskirts of the city. The dilapidated warehouses stood like forgotten sentinels, their windows shattered and walls covered in graffiti. Each step he took echoed through the desolate streets, a somber reminder of the desolation that permeated the area.

Sam's senses sharpened as he reached the entrance of the warehouse, his heart pounding with a mix of anticipation and caution. He could feel the weight of the night pressing down on him, the darkness seemingly alive with hidden dangers.

Pushing open the rusted door, he stepped into the cavernous space. The air was heavy with the scent of dampness and decay, and the only sound was the distant dripping of water. Sam's footsteps echoed, reverberating through the vast emptiness as he navigated his way deeper into the heart of The Baron's domain.

As he moved cautiously through the maze of corridors, he couldn't shake the feeling of being watched. Shadows danced on the walls, their elongated forms casting eerie silhouettes. The tension coiled within him, his instincts honed to their sharpest.

Suddenly, a noise broke the silence—a soft creak of floorboards. Sam froze, his hand instinctively reaching for the gun holstered at his side. He pressed himself against the cold brick wall, blending into the darkness, his eyes scanning the area.

A figure emerged from the shadows—a woman dressed in a sleek black dress that clung to her curves like a second skin. Her piercing green eyes glinted with a mix of curiosity and danger as she appraised Sam.

"I've been expecting you, Mr. Spade," she purred, her voice laced with a hint of mischief. "Word travels fast in this city."

Sam's grip tightened on his gun, his eyes never leaving the woman. "Who are you?"

She smiled, her lips curling into a sly grin. "They call me Viper," she replied, her voice dripping with an air of confidence. "I serve The Baron."

Sam's mind raced, considering his options. He knew he couldn't trust Viper, not when she stood in allegiance to his primary target. But he also recognized an opportunity—an opportunity to gather information, to peel back another layer of the twisted tapestry that enveloped Elena's disappearance.

"And what does The Baron want with me?" Sam asked, his voice steady despite the adrenaline coursing through his veins.

Viper's laughter echoed through the empty warehouse, bouncing off the walls. "The Baron is intrigued by your relentless pursuit of Elena," she said, her eyes glimmering with intrigue. "He wishes to meet you, to see what kind of man would dare challenge his reign."

Sam's jaw tightened. He had no illusions about the danger that awaited him. But if he wanted to find Elena and expose the truth, he would have to face The Baron head-on, even if it meant playing a dangerous game with Viper as his guide.

"Lead the way," Sam said, his voice laced with a quiet resolve. "But know this—I won't rest until I find Elena and unravel the darkness that shrouds this city."

Viper's smile widened, revealing a glimmer of admiration beneath her calculated demeanor. "Oh, Mr. Spade, you have no idea what you're stepping into. But I assure you, the truth you seek will reveal itself in due time."

And with that, Viper turned and led Sam further into the depths of the warehouse, where secrets whispered and shadows held the keys to unraveling a twisted conspiracy.

Chapter 4: The Baron's Lair

The journey through the warehouse was a treacherous dance with danger. Sam trailed behind Viper, his senses heightened, ready to react to any threat that lurked in the shadows. Every step brought them deeper into the heart of The Baron's domain, the air thick with an undercurrent of menace.

As they ventured further, the atmosphere grew more oppressive. The flickering light bulbs hanging from the ceiling cast eerie shadows that seemed to twist and contort with each passing moment. Sam couldn't help but feel like a pawn in a game whose rules he had yet to uncover.

Finally, they reached a heavy steel door, guarded by two imposing figures. Their presence exuded an aura of unquestionable loyalty to The Baron. Viper exchanged a few words with them in hushed tones before they reluctantly stepped aside, allowing Sam and Viper to pass.

The room beyond the door was bathed in an ethereal glow, its walls adorned with intricate tapestries that seemed to depict scenes of both opulence and deceit. The Baron's lair was a juxtaposition of power and darkness, a sanctuary where he ruled over his domain with an iron fist.

Seated at a grand desk, bathed in the warm glow of a crystal chandelier, was The Baron himself. His piercing eyes locked onto Sam, filled with a mix of curiosity and contempt. The room fell silent as the two men's gazes met, an unspoken challenge passing between them.

"Samuel Spade," The Baron's voice boomed, resonating with authority. "Your reputation precedes you. I must admit, I am impressed by your relentless pursuit of the truth."

Sam approached the desk, his expression a mask of determination. "Cut the pleasantries, Baron. I'm not here to exchange pleasantries. I want to know what you've done with Elena."

A wry smile tugged at The Baron's lips, his eyes gleaming with amusement. "Ah, Elena. Such a fascinating woman. She has a talent for finding trouble, doesn't she?"

Sam's grip tightened on the edge of the desk, his knuckles turning white. "Tell me where she is, Baron. I won't ask again."

The Baron leaned back in his chair, his gaze unwavering. "You see, Mr. Spade, Elena stumbled upon something she shouldn't have. She discovered a secret that could bring this city to its knees. And that's not something I can allow."

"And what is this secret?" Sam pressed, his voice low and dangerous.

The Baron's smile widened. "That, my dear detective, is for me to know and for you to find out. Consider this a game, Mr. Spade. If you can navigate the treacherous path I've laid out for you, perhaps you'll uncover the truth. But be warned, the stakes are high, and the consequences of failure are grave."

Sam's jaw clenched, his eyes burning with determination. He knew he was walking a dangerous tightrope, but he had come too far to turn back now. Elena's fate rested on his shoulders, and he would stop at nothing to uncover the truth and bring those responsible to justice.

"Very well, Baron," Sam said, his voice laced with resolve. "Consider me a player in your twisted game. But remember, I play to win."

With that, Sam turned on his heel, leaving The Baron and his lair behind. He had stepped deeper into the darkness, but little did he know that the true test of his mettle was yet to come.

Chapter 5: The Web Unraveled

Leaving The Baron's lair behind, Sam emerged into the night, his mind racing with the weight of the information he had gathered. The Baron's cryptic words echoed in his thoughts, each syllable a puzzle piece waiting to be solved.

As he stepped back into the rain-soaked streets, Sam's focus sharpened. He knew he needed to dig deeper, follow the twisted threads that led to Elena's disappearance and the secret she had uncovered. With each passing moment, the urgency to unravel the web of deceit intensified.

Returning to his office, Sam sifted through the scattered pieces of the puzzle. The rain continued to tap against the windowpane, a constant reminder of the world outside, cloaked in darkness and danger. He pushed aside his exhaustion, his determination driving him forward.

Sam retraced Elena's steps, studying every clue she left behind. He revisited the last places she had been seen, interviewing anyone who may have crossed paths with her. From rundown bars to opulent mansions, Sam pursued every lead with relentless persistence. The investigation had become a race against time, with the lives of both Elena and countless others hanging in the balance.

Days turned into nights, and Sam delved into the underbelly of the city, forging alliances with unlikely allies and navigating dangerous territories. He frequented smoke-filled jazz clubs where whispers of corruption mingled with the melodies, and he confronted seedy informants who traded in secrets like currency.

With each encounter, Sam pieced together a mosaic of deceit and power. The web of corruption he uncovered stretched far and wide, ensnaring politicians, police officials, and influential businessmen. The more he dug, the clearer it became that Elena's disappearance was connected to something much larger than he had initially imagined—a web of corruption that extended its insidious reach into the highest echelons of power.

Sam's investigations took him to the dimly lit offices of powerful corporations and the backrooms of illicit gambling dens. He uncovered secret transactions, hidden agendas, and the lengths to which those in power would go to protect their interests. The city itself seemed to pulse with a dark energy, its heart corrupted by the greed and malice that thrived beneath the surface.

Chapter 6: Unmasking the Puppet Master

As Sam delved deeper into the underbelly of the city, he became increasingly aware of the shadows that lurked around every corner. The rain-soaked streets whispered secrets, and the flickering neon lights cast an eerie glow on the faces of those who dared to venture out into the night. The city itself seemed alive, pulsating with a dark energy that fueled the corruption and malice that ran rampant.

His investigations led him to the dimly lit offices of a powerful corporation known as Evergreen Enterprises. With a reputation for shady dealings, it was rumored to be the puppet master behind much of the city's corruption. Sam had heard whispers of their involvement in everything from money laundering to illegal arms trading. Now, armed with evidence and determination, he intended to expose their dark secrets.

Disguised as a janitor, Sam infiltrated Evergreen Enterprises, navigating the labyrinthine corridors and evading the watchful eyes of security. The air hung heavy with tension as he made his way to the executive floor, where the true power resided. His heart pounded in his chest, every step bringing him closer to the heart of the web he had been untangling.

Reaching his destination, Sam found himself face to face with the imposing figure of Harold Denton, the CEO of Evergreen Enterprises. Denton's eyes bore into Sam's, their intensity matched only by the weight of his presence. The room was filled with an aura of power and menace as Sam confronted the man at the center of the tangled web.

Denton's voice was laced with cold amusement as he spoke, "Ah, Mr. Spade, what a surprise. I've been expecting you. It seems you've been quite persistent in your little investigation."

Sam's gaze remained steady, undeterred by Denton's attempt to intimidate him. "You can't hide forever, Denton. The city's secrets are unraveling, and your role in all of this will be exposed."

A sly smile curved Denton's lips. "Oh, Mr. Spade, you underestimate the power I wield. The city bends to my will, and no amount of digging will change that."

With a swift motion, Sam produced the evidence he had gathered, laying it on Denton's desk. "I have proof of your involvement in illegal activities, Denton. This city deserves justice, and I intend to ensure it gets it."

Denton's eyes flickered as he glanced at the incriminating documents before him. A hint of uncertainty crossed his face, but it quickly vanished, replaced by a mask of confidence. "You think a few pieces of paper can bring me down? You don't understand the depths of power at play here, Mr. Spade. I have friends in high places who will protect me."

Sam's voice hardened. "Your friends won't be able to shield you from the truth. The people deserve to know the extent of your corruption, Denton. Your reign ends here."

As the standoff continued, the room seemed to pulsate with tension. Sam knew that confronting Denton was a dangerous game, one that could have dire consequences. But he also understood that he couldn't turn away, not when the city's soul was at stake.

Suddenly, the sound of approaching footsteps broke the silence. The door swung open, revealing a group of armed guards, their eyes filled with steely determination. Denton's triumphant smile returned, and Sam realized he had walked right into a trap.

"It's over, Mr. Spade," Denton sneered, relishing the moment. "You thought you could bring me down, but you've merely sealed your own fate."

Sam's mind raced as he assessed the dire situation he found himself in. Surrounded by armed guards and facing an adversary as ruthless as Denton, he knew his options were limited. But Sam was no stranger to adversity, and he refused to surrender without a fight.

With a calm yet defiant gaze, Sam locked eyes with Denton. "You may have me cornered for now, Denton, but the truth has a way of surfacing. And when it does, you and your corrupt empire will crumble."

Denton's laughter echoed through the room, a chilling sound that sent shivers down Sam's spine. "Oh, Mr. Spade, you underestimate the power I hold. You think the truth matters in this city? The truth is what I say it is."

As Denton spoke, Sam's sharp instincts kicked in. He noticed a subtle shift in the guards' postures, a hint of unease in their eyes. His years of experience as a private investigator taught him to read people, to sense the cracks in their facade. And in that moment, he realized that not all was lost.

Sam's mind raced, searching for an escape plan, an opportunity to turn the tables. He glanced around the room, assessing his surroundings. The dimly lit office held potential hiding spots, but he needed a distraction—an opening to seize control of the situation.

Suddenly, a loud crash reverberated through the room as the office door swung open once again. Startled, the guards turned their attention towards the entrance, momentarily diverting their focus from Sam. In that split second, he seized the opportunity.

With lightning speed, Sam lunged forward, delivering a swift kick to the nearest guard, sending him sprawling to the ground. He deftly dodged the other guards' gunfire, using the office furniture as cover. With precise movements honed by years of experience, he disarmed one of the guards, snatching the weapon from his grasp.

Chaos erupted in the room as Sam fought back, each move calculated and precise. He utilized the element of surprise to his advantage, taking down the guards one by one. The stalemate had shifted in his favor, and the tide of the battle turned.

Denton, realizing his carefully crafted plan was unraveling, scrambled for an exit. But Sam, fueled by his unwavering pursuit of justice, pursued him relentlessly. Through a deadly game of cat and mouse, they weaved their way through the maze-like corridors of Evergreen Enterprises, their footsteps echoing against the cold, tiled floors.

As they reached the building's rooftop, the rain poured down in torrents, the storm mirroring the intensity of their confrontation. Sam cornered Denton, his breath ragged, his determination unyielding. The city skyline stretched before them, a backdrop to their final showdown.

"You can't escape the truth, Denton," Sam growled, his voice filled with conviction. "The web of corruption you've spun will crumble, and justice will prevail."

Denton's eyes burned with a mix of desperation and fury. "You think you've won, Mr. Spade? This city belongs to me, and I won't let you destroy everything I've built."

But Sam stood firm, his resolve unshakable. "You've underestimated the power of the people, Denton. The truth will come to light, and your reign of corruption will end."

With a final surge of determination, Sam lunged forward, his fists clenched. The two adversaries clashed, their struggle against the backdrop of the stormy night. Lightning streaked across the darkened sky, illuminating the rooftop with a brief, electric glow. Sam and Denton exchanged blows, their fight a fierce dance of strength and will. Rainwater mixed with the sweat on their brows as they grappled with each other, neither willing to yield.

Sam's training and relentless determination gave him an edge, but Denton's underhanded tactics and desperation made him a formidable opponent. Blow after blow was exchanged, the sound of their fists colliding echoing through the stormy night. Sam's mind was focused, channeling all his energy into defeating Denton and exposing the truth.

With a surge of adrenaline, Sam managed to deliver a powerful strike, sending Denton sprawling backward. The CEO's face contorted with rage and disbelief as he struggled to regain his footing. But before he could mount a counterattack, a sharp crack filled the air, followed by a blinding flash of lightning.

Denton's eyes widened in horror as the lightning struck a nearby antenna, its electric charge arcing through the air. In that split second, Sam seized the opportunity, swiftly grabbing Denton and pulling him towards the edge of the rooftop.

"You've run out of options, Denton," Sam declared, his voice cutting through the wind and rain. "It's time for the truth to be exposed."

Denton's grip weakened as he realized the perilous position he was in. The cityscape stretched out before them, a symbol of the world Denton had manipulated and controlled for far too long. Sam held Denton at the precipice, the storm raging around them, mirroring the storm of corruption Denton had wrought upon the city.

As the winds howled, Sam's grip tightened, forcing Denton to confront the consequences of his actions. "The city will no longer be held hostage by your corruption. It's time for justice, Denton."

Denton's eyes darted between the drop below and Sam's unwavering gaze. Fear and defeat mingled on his face as the weight of his crimes bore down upon him. With a final surge of strength, Sam pushed Denton back from the edge, ensuring his capture and the end of his reign.

Breathing heavily, Sam stood alone on the rain-soaked rooftop, the storm gradually subsiding. The battle was won, but the war against corruption was far from over. As the rainwater washed away the grime and deceit, Sam knew that his work had only just begun.

In the distance, sirens wailed, signaling the arrival of law enforcement to apprehend Denton and dismantle his corrupt empire. Sam knew that his actions had set in motion a chain of events that would reverberate throughout the city, exposing the web of corruption and giving hope to those who had long suffered under its shadow.

But as the rain washed away the stains of the past, Sam realized that the journey to justice was a marathon, not a sprint. The city would continue to face challenges, and new threats would emerge from the darkness. Yet, armed with the truth and his unwavering commitment, Sam vowed to be the relentless force that stood against the corrupt, the voice for the voiceless.

Under the fading storm clouds, Sam surveyed the cityscape with a renewed sense of purpose. The rain had cleansed the city, and though scars remained, a glimmer of hope emerged. It was a new chapter for the city, one where the truth would no longer be silenced, and where justice would prevail.

As the first rays of dawn broke through the dissipating clouds, Sam turned his gaze toward the horizon. The journey ahead was uncertain, but he was ready to face whatever challenges awaited him, one step at a time. The city needed its heroes, and Sam Spade was determined to be one of them. With a resolute spirit and the weight of the truth on his shoulders, Sam descended from the rooftop, ready to confront the aftermath of his battle against Denton and continue his relentless pursuit of justice.

Chapter 7: The Labyrinth Unveiled

The city had weathered the storm, both literally and metaphorically, but the aftermath of Sam's clash with Denton left lingering questions and a palpable tension in the air. The encounter had exposed a dangerous web of corruption, woven intricately within the city's power structures.

As Sam picked up the pieces of his shattered investigation, he knew he couldn't trust anyone. The line between friend and foe had blurred, and shadows of betrayal lurked in every corner. He had to tread carefully, for the stakes had never been higher.

Seeking solace and information, Sam found himself at the doorstep of an old informant, Maxine. Her rundown apartment was a refuge for those who danced on the fringes of society, and she possessed a wealth of knowledge about the city's underbelly.

Maxine, a woman hardened by life's trials, greeted Sam with a mix of wariness and curiosity. She knew better than to trust anyone blindly, especially a man entangled in the dangerous game of secrets and lies. But something about Sam's resolve sparked a glimmer of hope within her.

Over a cup of lukewarm coffee, Maxine shared what she knew—a clandestine organization called "The Syndicate" wielded immense power and controlled the strings behind the city's darkest operations. They were puppet masters, pulling the strings from the shadows, and Denton was merely a pawn in their grand scheme.

Sam's jaw tightened as he listened, his mind racing to connect the dots. The Syndicate's influence extended far and wide, infiltrating the police force, the judiciary, and even the highest echelons of politics. The corruption ran deep, and uncovering the truth meant putting his life on the line.

Armed with this new knowledge, Sam realized that he had become a threat to The Syndicate. He had pried too deeply into their affairs, exposing their secrets and disrupting their carefully constructed web. They would stop at nothing to silence him and protect their empire.

With the weight of impending danger pressing upon him, Sam devised a plan. He would gather evidence, piece together the puzzle of The Syndicate's operations, and expose them to the world. It was a race against time, for he knew that every step he took would bring him closer to the heart of darkness.

But as the walls closed in around him, Sam couldn't shake the feeling that someone close to him had already been compromised. The tendrils of betrayal snaked through the very fabric of his existence, and he couldn't afford to trust even his own reflection.

The rain poured outside, its rhythmic patter against the windowpane a constant reminder of the storm brewing within Sam's soul. Determined and fueled by a desire for justice, he steeled himself for the treacherous journey that lay ahead.

In the depths of the city's underbelly, where shadows whispered secrets and the truth had a price, Sam Spade would confront his demons head-on. The battle for the city's soul had just begun, and the outcome would determine not only his fate but the fate of all those ensnared in The Syndicate's grip.

With resolve burning in his eyes, Sam stepped out into the rain-soaked streets once again, ready to face the darkness and expose the truth that would bring the mighty Syndicate to its knees.

Chapter 8: Whispers in the Dark

The rain continued to pour relentlessly, drenching the city in a shroud of melancholy. Sam Spade, his coat collars turned up against the downpour, trudged through the sodden streets, his mind consumed by the events that had unfolded. The encounter with Denton had left him shaken, but it had also ignited a fire within him—an unwavering determination to expose the truth.

As Sam made his way back to his office, he couldn't shake the feeling of being watched. The shadows seemed to stretch and contort, concealing unseen eyes that followed his every move. Paranoia seeped into his bones, reminding him that he was treading dangerous waters. But he was no stranger to danger; it was an old companion that he had learned to dance with.

Entering the dimly lit office, Sam locked the door behind him, ensuring that he was shielded from prying eyes and listening ears. He needed a moment to gather his thoughts, to sift through the fragments of information he had gathered thus far. His investigation had unearthed a labyrinth of corruption, deceit, and power plays that reached far deeper than he had anticipated.

As he sat at his cluttered desk, the rain pelting against the window, Sam's gaze settled on a photograph of a woman—a woman whose fate was entwined with the darkness he sought to illuminate. Her name was Evelyn Sinclair, an enigmatic figure who had disappeared under mysterious circumstances. She was the key to unraveling the web of intrigue that had ensnared him.

Sam's mind raced, connecting the dots, and he realized that Denton's involvement in Evelyn's disappearance was no coincidence. There was a greater conspiracy at play, a hidden force manipulating the strings from the shadows. He couldn't trust anyone, not even his closest allies. The line between friend and foe had blurred, and he was navigating a treacherous path alone.

Driven by a dogged determination, Sam dug deeper into Evelyn's past, piecing together fragments of her life. Each clue he uncovered painted a darker picture, revealing a world of high-stakes politics, underground organizations, and a thirst for power that knew no bounds. The more he discovered, the more perilous his journey became.

But Sam was not one to cower in the face of danger. He had stared into the abyss before and emerged stronger. With every step he took, he grew closer to the heart of the conspiracy, inching closer to the truth that lay hidden in the shadows.

Little did Sam know that his relentless pursuit of justice would unleash forces that threatened to consume him entirely. The web of deceit he sought to untangle was far more intricate than he had ever imagined. As the rain continued to cascade outside, Sam prepared himself for the battles to come, knowing that the darkness he was about to confront would test him in ways he could scarcely comprehend.

Chapter 9: A Trail of Betrayal

The rain had finally subsided, leaving behind damp streets and a heavy atmosphere. Sam Spade stepped out of his office, his mind still consumed by the revelations that had unfolded in Chapter 8. He knew he was on the brink of uncovering a truth so profound it could rock the city to its core.

His investigation had led him to a hidden network of informants, each one possessing a fragment of the puzzle. With their help, Sam began piecing together the intricate web of deceit that surrounded Evelyn Sinclair's disappearance. As he delved deeper, he realized that the corruption reached far beyond Denton and his cohorts—it infiltrated the very fabric of society.

Sam's journey took him to the underbelly of the city, where the desperate and the destitute struggled to survive. He sought out those who lurked in the shadows, the ones who had seen the darkness firsthand. Their tales painted a chilling portrait of a city held captive by its own vices—a city where power reigned supreme, and morality was a luxury few could afford.

But with each revelation came a new betrayal. Trust became a scarce commodity as Sam discovered that even his most reliable sources had their own agendas. It seemed that everyone had something to hide, and loyalty was a fragile thread that threatened to snap at any moment.

As he navigated this treacherous landscape, Sam's path intersected with that of a mysterious figure known only as "The Whisperer." Rumors spoke of a man who possessed knowledge beyond measure, a man who held the key to unraveling the city's darkest secrets. Determined to find the truth, Sam embarked on a perilous journey to seek out this enigmatic figure.

The Whisperer dwelled in the heart of the city, hidden within a labyrinth of crumbling buildings and forgotten alleyways. Sam followed a series of cryptic clues that led him deeper into the maze, his senses heightened as he approached the elusive figure's lair.

Finally, Sam stood before a dilapidated door, weathered by time and neglect. He took a deep breath and pushed it open, entering a dimly lit chamber filled with whispers that seemed to echo from the walls themselves. There, seated at a weathered desk, was The Whisperer—a man draped in shadows, his face concealed beneath a tattered hood.

"The truth you seek is within your grasp," The Whisperer rasped, his voice a haunting melody that sent shivers down Sam's spine. "But be warned, for every answer comes with a price."

Sam's eyes narrowed, a steely resolve etching itself onto his features. He knew that he had come too far to turn back now. The Whisperer's words only fueled his determination to expose the corruption and bring justice to those who had been silenced.

"Tell me what you know," Sam demanded, his voice unwavering. "I will pay whatever price is required to uncover the truth."

The Whisperer leaned forward, his hood casting deeper shadows over his face. "Very well," he murmured, his voice laden with a mixture of foreboding and intrigue. "But remember, Sam Spade, some truths are best left buried."

Chapter 10: Shadows of the Past

The chamber fell into an eerie silence as Sam Spade absorbed The Whisperer's cryptic words. The weight of the truth he sought pressed upon him, mingling with a sense of foreboding. Determined to uncover the hidden secrets that plagued the city, he steeled himself for the journey ahead.

Leaving The Whisperer's chamber behind, Sam emerged into the night, where the city's neon lights flickered and cast distorted shadows on the rain-soaked pavement. The clues provided by The Whisperer led him deeper into the heart of the metropolis, where danger lurked in every alleyway and betrayal waited around every corner.

His investigation led him to a forgotten part of the city—an abandoned warehouse that reeked of decay and despair. As Sam cautiously stepped inside, his footsteps echoed through the desolate space, unsettling the silence that enveloped him. The air felt heavy with untold stories, as if the walls themselves held the secrets he sought.

In the dim light filtering through broken windows, Sam's keen eyes caught sight of a worn leather-bound journal lying amidst the debris. He carefully picked it up, the pages brittle with age. It belonged to Evelyn Sinclair, the woman whose disappearance had set this intricate chain of events into motion.

As he flipped through the journal's yellowed pages, Sam discovered a web of connections that ran deeper than he had ever imagined. Clues, half-formed thoughts, and cryptic scribbles hinted at a hidden power, a clandestine organization pulling the strings from the shadows. It became evident that Evelyn had stumbled upon something far more dangerous than anyone had anticipated.

Driven by a mix of curiosity and determination, Sam immersed himself in Evelyn's words, piecing together the fragments of her troubled mind. Her journal entries revealed a woman haunted by her own demons, caught in a web of deceit and manipulation. She had been on the brink of exposing the city's darkest secrets, but something had silenced her—a truth too dangerous to be revealed.

Sam's investigation took a perilous turn as he began to uncover connections between influential figures and their ties to this secret organization. The lines between friend and foe blurred, and he realized that no one could be trusted entirely. Even those he considered allies had hidden agendas, making the search for the truth a treacherous endeavor.

As he delved deeper into Evelyn's journal, Sam's path crossed with an old acquaintance, Detective Lydia Carter. They had once worked together, their paths intertwined in the pursuit of justice. Lydia, a woman with her own demons to confront, held valuable information that could help Sam unravel the mysteries that plagued the city.

Together, they formed an unlikely alliance, fueled by a shared determination to expose the truth and bring the hidden organization to its knees. With their combined skills and knowledge, they set out to infiltrate the labyrinthine network that lay beneath the city's surface, where corruption and power thrived.

Chapter 11: The Devil's Gambit

The rain poured relentlessly, drenching the city in a relentless downpour. Sam Spade and Detective Lydia Carter found themselves huddled in a dimly lit café, their faces obscured by shadows as they pored over the contents of Evelyn Sinclair's journal. The revelations within its pages had sent shockwaves through their investigation, exposing a network of corruption that reached the highest echelons of power.

As they exchanged theories and connected the dots, a name emerged—a name whispered in hushed tones among the city's underground circles: Damien Blackwood. He was a formidable figure, a man of wealth and influence, whose dark dealings remained shrouded in secrecy. Rumors swirled around him like smoke, painting a portrait of a puppet master manipulating the city's fate.

Driven by a shared determination, Sam and Lydia embarked on a relentless pursuit of Damien Blackwood. They delved into the city's underbelly, following the breadcrumbs left by Evelyn's journal. Each step drew them deeper into the tangled web of corruption, their every move shadowed by unseen eyes.

Their investigation led them to a lavish mansion nestled on the outskirts of the city—a fortress guarded by loyal henchmen and impenetrable walls. Sam and Lydia knew that their only chance of exposing the truth lay within those walls, no matter the risks they faced.

Under the cover of night, they infiltrated the mansion's grounds, moving like phantoms through the darkness. Evading security measures and silently disabling alarms, they made their way closer to the heart of Damien Blackwood's operation. The air crackled with tension as they crept through opulent halls, past rooms filled with secrets waiting to be unraveled.

Finally, they reached the inner sanctum—a hidden chamber adorned with symbols of power and wealth. A massive oak desk dominated the room, and behind it sat Damien Blackwood, a figure shrouded in darkness, his eyes gleaming with a sinister allure. He exuded an air of arrogance, as if he held all the strings in his hands.

"You've come far, Mr. Spade," Damien Blackwood spoke, his voice laced with cold amusement. "But I'm afraid your journey ends here."

Sam Spade and Lydia Carter stood their ground, their resolve unwavering. They had come too far to back down now. With a steady gaze, Sam replied, "We know what you've been doing, Blackwood. Your reign of corruption ends tonight."

A tense standoff ensued, with the weight of truth hanging heavily in the air. The room crackled with an invisible energy—a collision of wills, where the forces of justice clashed with the darkness that had consumed the city.

In that pivotal moment, Sam and Lydia realized that their battle was not merely against a single man but against an entire system built on lies and manipulation. They were fighting not only for the truth but also for the very soul of the city they loved.

With hearts pounding and adrenaline surging through their veins, they prepared to face the devil himself. The stage was set for a high-stakes confrontation—a battle that would determine the fate of not just Sam and Lydia, but of everyone entangled in the web of corruption.

The room fell into a heavy silence, tension hanging in the air like a taut wire. Damien Blackwood's gaze bore into Sam and Lydia, his expression morphing from amusement to a dangerous glint. Slowly, a smile curled at the corners of his lips, revealing a predator's satisfaction.

"You underestimate the power I hold, Mr. Spade," Blackwood hissed, his voice laced with venom. "In this city, I am the puppeteer, and you are mere pawns in my game."

Sam's eyes narrowed, a flicker of defiance igniting within him. He knew the odds were stacked against them, but he also understood that exposing Blackwood's web of deceit was their only chance at reclaiming justice. He exchanged a determined glance with Lydia, a silent understanding passing between them.

"We've seen the depths of your corruption, Blackwood," Sam retorted, his voice steady. "Your empire may be vast, but it's built on the suffering of innocents. We won't rest until we bring you down."

Blackwood's laughter echoed through the room, bouncing off the walls like a haunting melody. "Oh, how I enjoy your misplaced heroics," he sneered. "But mark my words, Mr. Spade, your crusade ends tonight. The city is mine, and nothing can stand in my way."

With a sudden motion, Blackwood pressed a concealed button on his desk, triggering a cascade of events. The floor beneath Sam and Lydia trembled as hidden mechanisms sprang to life. In an instant, the room transformed into a deathtrap, with walls closing in and concealed weapons emerging from hidden compartments.

Sam's mind raced, searching for a way out. The odds were grim, but he refused to give in. He scanned the room, his eyes landing on a ventilation shaft high above them. Without hesitation, he motioned to Lydia, pointing at their potential escape route.

"We need to get to that vent!" Sam shouted above the din of impending doom. "Now!"

They sprang into action, their bodies moving with practiced agility. Dodging laser beams and evading projectiles, they fought their way through the deadly maze. Inch by inch, they inched closer to their salvation, their determination eclipsing the fear that threatened to consume them.

Finally, with their backs against the wall and time running out, Sam and Lydia reached the ventilation shaft. Without a moment's hesitation, they scrambled up, the metallic grating biting into their palms as they pulled themselves through the narrow opening.

They emerged onto the rooftop, rain-soaked and gasping for breath. The storm raged around them, mirroring the tempest within their hearts. Blackwood's mansion loomed behind them, a symbol of the battles yet to be fought. They had escaped the jaws of the devil, but their mission was far from over.

As they stood under the tumultuous sky, Sam and Lydia shared a silent vow. They would regroup, gather their allies, and strike back at Blackwood's empire with everything they had. The city deserved redemption, and they would stop at nothing to deliver it.

Chapter 12: Into the Lion's Den

In the aftermath of their narrow escape from Blackwood's mansion, Sam and Lydia found refuge in a hidden safehouse, a sanctuary known only to a select few. The rain continued to pour relentlessly, drumming against the windows like an urgent plea for justice. They knew they couldn't waste a moment.

As they caught their breath, Sam's mind raced, trying to make sense of the revelations they had uncovered. The pieces of the puzzle were scattered before them, each fragment revealing a glimpse of the twisted tapestry they were unraveling. They pored over case files, surveillance footage, and cryptic messages, connecting dots and drawing lines that led to the heart of the conspiracy.

Their investigation had unveiled a network of corruption that extended far beyond Blackwood's individual deeds. It reached into the highest echelons of power, ensnaring influential figures whose influence shaped the city's destiny. Sam realized that to bring down Blackwood and restore justice, they would have to expose not just him but the entire rotten infrastructure that supported him.

But in this dangerous game, the line between ally and enemy blurred. Betrayal lurked around every corner, and Sam couldn't shake the feeling that they were being watched, that their every move was being monitored. The walls of the safehouse seemed to close in on them, suffocating their hopes of a swift victory.

Lydia, always astute and perceptive, broke the silence. "Sam, we can't do this alone. We need allies, people we can trust."

Sam nodded, acknowledging the truth in her words. They had to forge unlikely alliances, find those who had also been wronged by Blackwood's grip on the city. They needed a united front, a coalition of those who still believed in justice, even in the face of overwhelming odds.

Together, they compiled a list of names—the disgraced cop who had lost everything, the investigative journalist silenced by fear, the former enforcer seeking redemption. Each person had their own reasons to join the fight, their own scores to settle. Sam reached out to them, making connections in the shadows, treading carefully to avoid tipping off their enemies.

In the weeks that followed, the coalition grew, united by a shared desire to expose the truth and dismantle Blackwood's empire. They trained, strategized, and planned their next move. The safehouse buzzed with activity, its once empty rooms now filled with purpose and determination.

But even as they prepared to strike back, a new sense of urgency took hold. The city's grip tightened, its citizens suffocated by fear and oppression. Blackwood's reach extended further, infiltrating every aspect of their lives. The coalition knew they had to act swiftly, before hope completely dwindled and the city succumbed to darkness.

As the rain poured outside, Sam and Lydia stood at the heart of the safehouse, surrounded by the faces of those who had chosen to fight alongside them. They locked eyes, their gaze reflecting a shared resolve that nothing could break.

"We've come too far to turn back now," Sam said, his voice steady. "We will expose the shadows, confront the betrayal head-on, and bring justice to this city. Let the storm rage, for it will be the harbinger of our retribution."

And with those words, the coalition prepared to unleash a storm of their own, ready to challenge the forces that had conspired against them. In the face of treachery, their determination burned brighter, igniting a beacon of hope in the darkest of times.

Chapter 13: The Sinister Revelation

The rain had ceased, leaving the city drenched and glistening under the moon's pale light. Sam and Lydia, accompanied by their coalition, stood on the precipice of a new phase in their battle against Blackwood's reign of terror. They knew that the time for secrets and half-truths had passed; they had to confront the sinister revelation that awaited them.

Within the safehouse's dimly lit command center, they gathered around a large table strewn with maps, surveillance photos, and scraps of evidence. The coalition's collective effort had unearthed a pattern—a series of seemingly unrelated events that, when connected, pointed to a far more insidious truth.

Sam's finger traced a line across the map, connecting the locations where the crimes had occurred. Murders, disappearances, and cover-ups formed a web that sprawled across the city, its tendrils stretching into the heart of every major institution. Blackwood's influence permeated every corner, weaving a tapestry of corruption that left no stone unturned.

Lydia leaned in, her eyes scanning the evidence with a mix of determination and concern. "These incidents are just the tip of the iceberg," she said. "They're part of a grand design—a plan to exert control and manipulate the city's power dynamics."

Sam nodded, his jaw set with resolve. "Blackwood isn't just a criminal mastermind; he's a puppeteer pulling the strings behind the scenes. And we're about to expose his true intentions."

Their investigation had led them to a revelation that struck at the core of the city's foundation. Blackwood's ambitions went beyond personal gain or dominance. He sought to plunge the city into chaos, to orchestrate a web of fear and despair from which he would emerge as the ultimate puppet master.

But unraveling Blackwood's intricate plan required more than connecting the dots. It demanded infiltrating the heart of his operations, where the true machinations unfolded. Sam turned to their coalition, addressing them with unwavering determination.

"We need to penetrate the heart of Blackwood's empire, expose his true intentions, and bring him down," he declared. "It won't be easy. We'll face unimaginable risks, but we can't allow fear to hold us back. Our mission is to restore justice and reclaim this city from the clutches of darkness."

The coalition nodded, their faces reflecting a mix of determination, apprehension, and unwavering resolve. They had come too far to back down now. Each member understood the magnitude of the task ahead—the sacrifices they would have to make, the secrets they would have to confront.

Days turned into nights as they meticulously planned their assault. They studied blueprints, identified weak points in Blackwood's organization, and gathered information that would expose his true agenda. It became clear that their operation would be a delicate dance between stealth and force, as they sought to dismantle his network and reveal the extent of his corruption.

As they prepared to embark on this dangerous endeavor, a sense of anticipation hung in the air—a palpable electricity that ignited their spirits. They were united by a singular purpose: to uncover the sinister truth, to dismantle Blackwood's empire, and to restore hope to the city's beleaguered souls.

Chapter 14: Racing Against Time

The city was a powder keg, teetering on the brink of destruction. Sam Spade and his coalition of truth-seekers were determined to expose Blackwood's sinister agenda before it was too late. With the clock ticking relentlessly, they knew they had to act swiftly, for time was their most precious commodity.

Their investigation had led them to an abandoned warehouse on the outskirts of the city—an inconspicuous stronghold where Blackwood conducted his most heinous operations. Armed with the knowledge they had acquired, Sam and his team stealthily approached the fortress of darkness, their hearts pounding in anticipation.

Under the cover of night, they infiltrated the warehouse, skillfully evading the watchful eyes of Blackwood's guards. As they made their way through the labyrinthine corridors, a sense of urgency enveloped them. Every step brought them closer to unraveling the web of deceit that held the city captive.

Whispers of conversations reached their ears—hushed discussions about the final phase of Blackwood's plan. The stakes were higher than they had ever imagined. Lives hung in the balance, and the city's fate teetered on a precipice of destruction.

Suddenly, they stumbled upon a hidden chamber—a secret vault that housed Blackwood's most guarded secrets. The room was filled with an array of technological marvels, each one a testament to Blackwood's insidious brilliance. Screens flickered with surveillance footage, revealing the extent of his influence. Plans, blueprints, and encrypted files lay strewn across the desks, waiting to be deciphered.

Sam's eyes narrowed as he surveyed the room, his mind racing with the weight of their discovery. They had stumbled upon the key to exposing Blackwood's true intentions, but time was slipping through their fingers. They had to retrieve the evidence, crack the code, and bring the truth to light before the city succumbed to the darkness that loomed overhead.

As the coalition split into teams, each member took on a vital role in deciphering the clues and gathering the evidence. Hours turned into minutes as they raced against time, their fingers flying across keyboards, their minds working at an unprecedented pace. The room buzzed with intensity, the air thick with the determination of those who refused to let evil prevail.

Finally, as the final seconds ticked away, a breakthrough came. The encrypted files yielded their secrets, and the truth was laid bare before them. Blackwood's plan was far more sinister than they had anticipated—a cataclysmic event that would plunge the city into chaos, leaving no survivors in its wake.

With the evidence in hand, Sam and his coalition retreated from the warehouse, their mission far from complete. They had the truth, but they had yet to expose it to the world. Blackwood's web of deceit extended far and wide, ensnaring those in positions of power and influence. They had to tread carefully, for their every move was under scrutiny.

Chapter 15: A Fragile Alliance

The weight of the truth hung heavy in the air as Sam Spade and his coalition prepared to expose Blackwood's sinister agenda. With the evidence in their possession, they knew they needed to forge alliances and gather support if they were to succeed in their mission. But in a city where loyalties were fragile and betrayal lurked at every corner, they had to tread carefully.

Sam reached out to a select few individuals he believed he could trust—people who had seen glimpses of the darkness that consumed the city and were willing to fight for its redemption. Together, they formed a fragile alliance, bound by their shared determination to expose the truth and bring down Blackwood.

In the dimly lit basement of an old speakeasy, the coalition gathered. Faces marked by weariness and resolve stared back at Sam as he addressed them, laying out the gravity of their task. Each member brought unique skills and connections to the table, but it was their collective commitment to justice that held them together.

Among the group was Lana, a skilled hacker with a deep-rooted hatred for Blackwood and a personal vendetta against him. Her nimble fingers danced across the keyboard, accessing classified information and ensuring their digital footprint remained invisible. She was their guardian in the shadows, shielding them from prying eyes and protecting their identities.

Next to her sat Marcus, a former detective with a reputation for being relentless. His knowledge of the city's underbelly and his network of contacts made him an invaluable asset. He was the one who could navigate the treacherous paths of corruption and provide the coalition with the necessary leverage to unravel Blackwood's web of influence.

Completing the alliance was Emily, a journalist with an unwavering commitment to the truth. Her words had the power to sway public opinion and expose the darkest secrets of the city's elite. With her pen as her sword, she would bring the fight to the front lines, using the power of the media to shed light on the corruption that had festered for far too long.

As the coalition strategized, Sam could sense the tension in the room. Each member had their own motives, their own pasts that fueled their determination. But he knew that unity was their greatest strength. They had to set aside their personal vendettas and work together, for only by combining their skills and resources could they hope to overcome Blackwood's formidable reach.

The path ahead was treacherous, and their every move would be met with resistance. Blackwood was a master manipulator, capable of turning allies into enemies with a single whisper. They had to be vigilant, watching for signs of infiltration and betrayal from within their ranks.

Sam Spade, the hardened private investigator, had become the glue that held the fragile alliance together. His unwavering determination and unwavering commitment to justice inspired those around him, even as doubts and fears threatened to seep into their hearts. He had seen the darkest depths of the city and emerged with his moral compass intact—a guiding light in the face of overwhelming darkness.

Chapter 16: Breaking Point

The alliance had been forged, but the pressure was mounting, pushing each member to their breaking point. As they delved deeper into their mission to expose Blackwood, cracks began to appear within the fragile unity they had established. The weight of their personal demons and the relentless pursuit of justice threatened to tear them apart.

Sam Spade found himself grappling with his own inner turmoil. The darkness he had encountered in the city mirrored the shadows that haunted his own past. Memories he had long tried to bury resurfaced, threatening to consume him. The lines between his quest for justice and his personal vendetta blurred, and he questioned if he could truly separate the two.

Lana, the hacker, became increasingly consumed by her burning desire for revenge against Blackwood. Her focus on dismantling his empire began to overshadow the well-being of the coalition. Her actions grew reckless, endangering the lives of those around her. The delicate balance between her skills and her personal vendetta was at the tipping point.

Marcus, once a beacon of unwavering determination, found himself wrestling with doubt. The weight of the city's corruption bore heavily on his shoulders, and he questioned if their efforts were in vain. The enormity of Blackwood's power threatened to crush his spirit, pushing him to the edge of despair. The line between conviction and futility blurred, and he wondered if they were merely scratching the surface of a much deeper and insidious plot.

Emily, the journalist, faced her own struggles as she encountered roadblocks in her pursuit of exposing the truth. Blackwood's influence extended far and wide, and her efforts to rally public support were met with resistance and threats. The integrity of her reporting was called into question, and she had to grapple with the fine line between journalistic ethics and the desperate need to bring down a corrupt empire.

The breaking point loomed, and tensions within the coalition reached a boiling point. Trust wavered, tempers flared, and doubts multiplied. It seemed as if the very foundation they had built their alliance upon was crumbling beneath them. Yet, it was precisely at this critical juncture that they needed to find strength in each other, to remember their shared purpose and the lives that hung in the balance.

In the face of adversity, they were forced to confront their own vulnerabilities and the consequences of their choices. It was a pivotal moment, a test of their resilience and determination. The breaking point could either shatter them or strengthen their resolve to overcome the obstacles ahead.

Chapter 17: The Final Showdown

The stage was set for the ultimate confrontation between the alliance and the insidious Blackwood. The city trembled with anticipation, its pulse quickening as the hour of reckoning approached. Each member of the coalition knew that this battle would determine the fate of not only their own lives but also the future of the city itself.

Sam Spade, hardened by years of chasing shadows and battling his inner demons, stood at the forefront. Determination burned in his eyes as he prepared to face Blackwood, the embodiment of corruption and power. The time for subtlety and investigation had passed; it was now a clash of wills, a clash of ideologies.

Lana, her fingers poised over her keyboard, unleashed a torrent of digital fury, probing the deepest recesses of Blackwood's networks. Her every keystroke was a weapon, and she aimed to dismantle his empire piece by piece. The binary battlefield mirrored the intensity of the physical confrontation to come.

Marcus, his resolve rekindled, stood tall beside Sam. His unwavering belief in justice and the fight against the corrupt inspired those around him. With every step he took, he carried the weight of the city's hopes and dreams, vowing to bring an end to the tyranny that had plagued their lives for far too long.

Emily, armed with the truth she had painstakingly uncovered, prepared to expose Blackwood's crimes to the world. Her words were a weapon sharper than any blade, ready to pierce through the layers of deception and pierce Blackwood's armor of lies. She knew that the power of information could topple even the mightiest of adversaries.

As the alliance approached Blackwood's fortress, the tension in the air was palpable. The echoes of their footsteps reverberated through the empty halls, each step a declaration of defiance against the darkness that had consumed the city. The final showdown was about to unfold, and there would be no turning back.

The confrontation erupted in a storm of fury and determination. Blackwood's forces, loyal to the core, clashed with the united front of the alliance. Fists flew, bullets whizzed through the air, and the battle raged on. It was a fight for justice, for redemption, and for the future of a city on the brink of collapse.

Amidst the chaos, alliances were tested, loyalties were questioned, and sacrifices were made. The members of the coalition faced their own personal demons while battling the physical manifestations of Blackwood's corruption. Each blow struck was a step closer to victory or defeat, their fates intertwined in a dance of desperation and resilience.

The final moments of the showdown drew near. Sam, bloodied and bruised, locked eyes with Blackwood, their gazes filled with the weight of their shared history. It was a moment of truth, where the sins of the past collided with the promise of a better future. One would emerge victorious, and the other would be consumed by the darkness they had embraced.

In the heart-pounding climax, the alliance fought with everything they had. They channeled their pain, their anger, and their unwavering belief in justice. It was a battle that transcended physicality, a battle fought on moral grounds. And in the end, as the dust settled and the smoke cleared, the outcome was determined.

Chapter 18: Confronting the Past

The city stood battered and bruised, its wounds reflecting the aftermath of the epic battle that had unfolded. The alliance, weary but resolute, had emerged victorious, shattering the grip of Blackwood's corruption and restoring a glimmer of hope to the desolate streets. Yet, as they surveyed the wreckage, a new challenge awaited them—a confrontation with their own pasts.

Sam Spade, his once impenetrable facade cracked by the weight of the recent events, found himself grappling with ghosts that had long haunted him. The echoes of his past misdeeds reverberated through his mind, demanding attention and resolution. He knew that in order to fully move forward, he had to face the demons that lurked within his own soul.

Driven by the need for closure, Sam embarked on a personal journey, retracing the steps that had led him down the treacherous path he had walked for so long. Each step brought him face to face with the consequences of his actions, the lives he had inadvertently shattered, and the choices that had shaped him into the man he had become.

Haunted by regret and seeking redemption, Sam sought solace in the unlikeliest of places—the graveyard where his former partner, Max, lay at rest. Standing before the weathered tombstone, he poured out his heart, confessing his sins, and seeking forgiveness from the one person who had believed in him when no one else had.

Meanwhile, Lana, the brilliant hacker with a troubled past of her own, found herself tormented by the shadows that refused to let her go. The secrets she had buried deep within her threatened to resurface, threatening the fragile alliance she had forged. With the battle won, she had to confront her own vulnerabilities and face the truth that had long eluded her.

In the quiet solitude of her apartment, Lana delved into her past, unearthing painful memories and buried truths. Each revelation chipped away at the walls she had erected, exposing her vulnerabilities. But through the darkness, she discovered a newfound strength—a resilience that would carry her through the storm of her own making.

Together, Sam and Lana embarked on a shared journey of self-discovery and redemption, intertwining their stories as they confronted their pasts head-on. The bond between them grew stronger, forged through the fire of adversity and their mutual determination to leave the shadows behind.

As they unraveled the tangled threads of their histories, Sam and Lana realized that confronting the past was not about erasing it or seeking absolution. It was about acknowledging the mistakes, the pain, and the scars, and finding the strength to move forward, armed with newfound wisdom and a renewed sense of purpose.

Chapter 19: Redemption and Sacrifice

T he city breathed a collective sigh of relief as dawn broke over the horizon, casting a gentle light on the scars that marred its streets. The battle against Blackwood's reign of terror had exacted a heavy toll, leaving behind a landscape of broken dreams and shattered lives. But amidst the wreckage, a glimmer of hope remained, fueled by the resilience and courage of those who had fought to reclaim their city.

Sam Spade and Lana stood at the crossroads of their intertwined destinies, their pasts laid bare before them. The weight of their actions, both good and bad, bore down on their shoulders, but they carried it with newfound purpose. Redemption beckoned, a chance to right the wrongs of their past and forge a path towards a brighter future.

For Sam, redemption meant more than just atoning for his sins; it meant protecting those he held dear and preserving the fragile balance of justice in a world tainted by corruption. He knew that sacrifices had to be made, that sometimes the line between right and wrong blurred in the face of greater evils. With each step he took, he carried the weight of his choices, guided by a moral compass that burned brighter than ever before.

Lana, too, embraced the call for redemption. Her journey had brought her face to face with the darkness that had threatened to consume her. But she refused to let her past define her future. With unwavering determination, she vowed to use her skills to bring light to the shadows, to expose the truth and dismantle the webs of deceit that ensnared innocent lives. In doing so, she sought to find her own redemption, a chance to rewrite her story and prove that her actions could shape a better world.

As the city grappled with the aftermath of the battle, Sam and Lana joined forces once again, their paths converging in a final, decisive act of sacrifice. They understood that the fight against evil required not only physical strength but also the willingness to give up something precious, to lay it all on the line for the greater good.

Their alliance became a beacon of hope for a city in desperate need of heroes. They rallied those who had suffered under Blackwood's tyranny, inspiring them to rise up and join the cause. Together, they formed an army of resilience and defiance, ready to face whatever lay ahead.

In the heart of the city, at the very center of Blackwood's stronghold, Sam and Lana stood face to face with their nemesis. It was a battle not just of fists and bullets, but of ideologies and values. They fought with unwavering determination, drawing upon their past experiences, their pain, and their newfound sense of purpose.

And as the final blow was struck, and Blackwood's empire crumbled, Sam and Lana knew that their redemption had come at a price. They had sacrificed pieces of themselves along the way, shedding their old selves to become something greater. In the wake of their victory, they found solace in the knowledge that their actions had made a difference, that their sacrifices had not been in vain.

Chapter 20: A New Beginning

The sun climbed higher in the sky, casting a golden glow over the city's rejuvenated streets. The remnants of Blackwood's reign were being swept away, replaced by a newfound sense of optimism and possibility. Sam Spade and Lana, their shared journey having forged an unbreakable bond, stood on the precipice of a new chapter in their lives.

The once dimly lit office that had served as Sam's sanctuary had undergone a transformation. The stale cigarette smoke had dissipated, replaced by the scent of fresh beginnings. The room was now bathed in natural light, the dust of the past wiped clean. It mirrored the change within Sam and Lana themselves, a testament to their resilience and the hope that now burned brightly within their hearts.

Together, they had emerged from the crucible of darkness, stronger and wiser than before. They had witnessed the depths of humanity's capacity for evil, but they had also seen the flickers of light that could guide them towards a better future. Their shared experiences had shaped them into something more than just individuals; they had become beacons of justice, symbols of hope for a city in need of redemption.

As the final embers of the past were extinguished, Sam and Lana turned their attention to the future. They knew that the work was far from over, that there would always be new battles to fight and injustices to right. But they were prepared. Armed with the lessons learned from their journey, they were ready to face whatever challenges lay ahead.

Their private investigation agency, once a mere refuge for lost souls, now stood as a testament to their unwavering commitment to truth and justice. It became a beacon for those seeking help, a sanctuary where the vulnerable could find solace and the guilty could face their reckoning. Sam and Lana had earned their place as defenders of the innocent, their names whispered with gratitude and respect throughout the city.

And as they stepped out onto the bustling streets, the city greeted them with open arms. Strangers nodded in acknowledgment, acknowledging the heroes who had restored their faith in humanity. The rain-soaked city streets that had once glistened with a sense of foreboding now shimmered with a newfound optimism. The ghosts of the past had been laid to rest, and the city had begun to heal.

Sam and Lana, their paths forever entwined, walked side by side, ready to embrace the challenges and mysteries that awaited them. They knew that their journey had been more than just a pursuit of truth; it had been a journey of self-discovery, redemption, and the unbreakable bond forged in the crucible of darkness.

In the distance, a storm brewed, its dark clouds a reminder of the challenges that lay ahead. But Sam and Lana faced it with determination, for they knew that they had each other and the unwavering support of a city that believed in their cause. The rain began to fall, but they welcomed it, knowing that every drop carried the promise of a brighter future.

And so, as they ventured forward, their footsteps echoing on the rain-soaked pavement, Sam and Lana embraced the uncertainty of their new beginning. They were ready to navigate the intricate dance between shadows and light, to unravel the mysteries that lay hidden beneath the surface. Their journey had only just begun, but with hearts alight with purpose, they walked forward, united in their quest for truth, justice, and the eternal pursuit of redemption.

The end marks a new beginning.